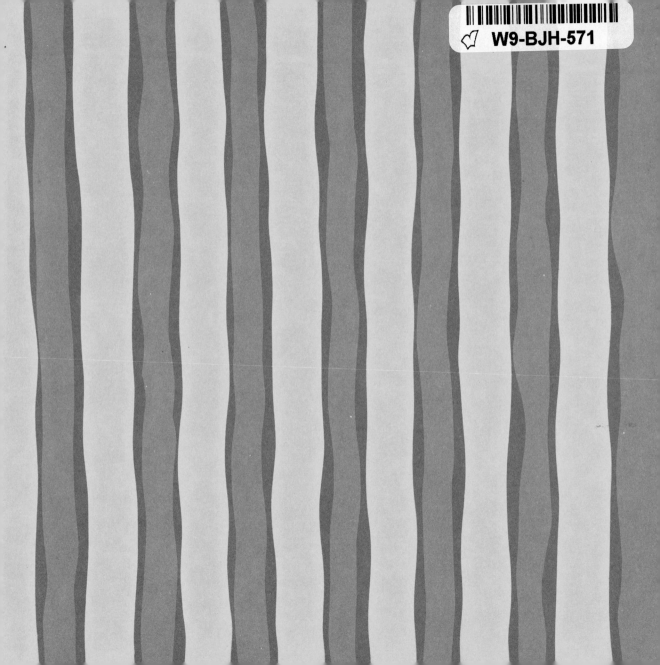

Theodore

by Edward Ormondroyd
illustrated by John M. Larrecq

Parnassus Press   Oakland   California
Houghton Mifflin Company   Boston

for
Evan, who acts
like a bear
Beth, a blue bear
Kitt, who prefers
cats; and for
Andrea and
Matthew

Lucy really loved her bear, Theodore, but sometimes she was careless with him. Theodore didn't mind. He was an old experienced bear, comfortably smudgy, who knew that it was part of life to be forgotten now and then in a closet or under the cellar stairs. And Lucy always made it up to him with

something special. She would take him to bed, or give him a tea party which made him more comfortably smudgy than ever, with jam in his fur.

'She may be careless now and then,' Theodore thought, 'but she understands bears.'

One morning Lucy tried to dress Theodore in her pyjamas. They were much too big for him. She went outside to play, leaving Theodore on the floor buried in pyjamas.

"Honestly, that girl!" said Lucy's mother when she looked into Lucy's room. "When is she *ever* going to learn to pick up her clothes?" She collected pants, shirts, socks and underwear, tossing them on top of the pyjamas, and then scrunched them all up together. She didn't notice that Theodore was inside

the bundle. She dropped the clothes in the laundry
basket.

'Ho hum', Theodore thought, after several days

in the laundry basket. 'Being a bear is a comfortable
life, but a little dull sometimes. I guess I might as well
take a nap until Lucy finds me again.'

Theodore dreamed that Lucy took him up for a
ride in an airplane. But she was careless, and forgot
to strap him in. While she was showing him how to
do an inside loop, he fell out.

'Now, *wait* a minute!' Theodore thought as he
tumbled over and over. 'This is no situation for a bear
to be in. I'd better wake up.'

He did wake up. But he was still tumbling over

and over. The clothes were tumbling around with him. Every few seconds he could catch a quick look through a round window. On the other side of the window were Lucy's father and some other people, sitting in a row and reading magazines. The horrible truth came to him: *he was inside a washing machine at the self-service laundry!*

'Help!' cried Theodore in a bubbly voice, as water poured in around him.

Theodore couldn't think very clearly during the next half hour, but he knew that he would much rather fall out of an airplane than be washed like this. He was soused around and around in very hot water. Soap suds got into his eyes and ears. Buttons

and zippers banged him on the nose. When the machine went into its final spin he almost blacked out.

'Oh my!' Theodore mumbled damply when everything was still and quiet again. 'Thank goodness that's all!'

But that wasn't all.

Lucy's father didn't know the right way to do laundry, or he would have found Theodore. He pulled all the clothes out of the washer in a wad, and without separating them or shaking them out, he threw them into the drying machine. *Rumble tumble, rumble tumble*—Theodore found himself being tossed around in a fierce blast of heat. He cried 'Help, help!' in a feeble voice, and fainted.

When he came to again he was buried in red-hot clothes. 'Must—get—some—air', he gasped, beginning to struggle. Lucy's father was pulling the laundry basket on Lucy's express wagon, and the jolting helped Theodore to fight his way free. He hung over the edge of the basket, trying to get back his breath. Suddenly the wagon bounced over a curb, and Theodore fell out on the sidewalk.

In a few minutes he revived enough to sit up. What a shock when he looked down at his arms and legs! His fur was so shiny and golden and fluffy that he couldn't recognize himself.

'Hmmm', he thought. 'This doesn't look like me. It doesn't feel right, either. It doesn't feel *bearish* . . . Ah! Here comes Lucy. Now everything will be all right!'

Lucy rode up quickly on her tricycle, and then stopped and shook her head. "A new bear," she said sadly. "I thought it was Theodore."

'It *is* me!' Theodore squeaked. But Lucy had begun to ride away, and she didn't hear him.

'I knew it!' said Theodore to himself. 'It's *dangerous* for a bear to be this clean. Something must be done!'

Just then a dog came trotting by.

'May I beg your assistance, sir?' Theodore asked.

The friendly dog obliged by dragging him through the gutter for a while, and then left him in a freshly-spaded flower bed. 'Thank you,' said Theodore. 'I'm feeling more bearish already.'

Two tomcats began to yowl at each other under the bushes nearby.

'Allow me to join in your dispute, gentlemen,' Theodore said.

The cats obliged by fighting each other with Theodore in between. He was thoroughly scrubbed around in the dirt, and some of his fur was clawed off. 'Thank you', said Theodore. 'This is a vast improvement'.

A little boy with a taffy sucker found him next.

'Would you consider sharing that with me, young man?' Theodore asked.

The little boy obliged by trying to feed Theodore his sucker. When he was through, Theodore was very gummy around the ears, and his paws were stuck together. 'Thank you', said Theodore. 'This feels just like old times again. Ah, here comes Lucy!'

"Theodore!" Lucy cried "Where have you been, you naughty bear? I've been looking all over for you for days!"

She scolded him all the way home. Theodore loved it.

"Look!" Lucy shouted to her mother. "I found Theodore again!"

"That's nice," said Lucy's mother. "My goodness, he's dirtier than ever. I have an idea: why don't you let me take him to the laundry next week and run him through with the clothes?"

'Oh *no*!' Theodore thought.

Lucy considered a moment.

"No," she said finally. "I saw a new clean bear a little while ago, and he didn't look happy. See how happy Theodore looks? He *likes* being smudgy."

"Oh, all right," said Lucy's mother. "It's your bear."

'Well', Theodore thought with a tremendous sigh of relief, as he and Lucy hugged each other, 'she may be careless at times, but she *does* understand bears'.

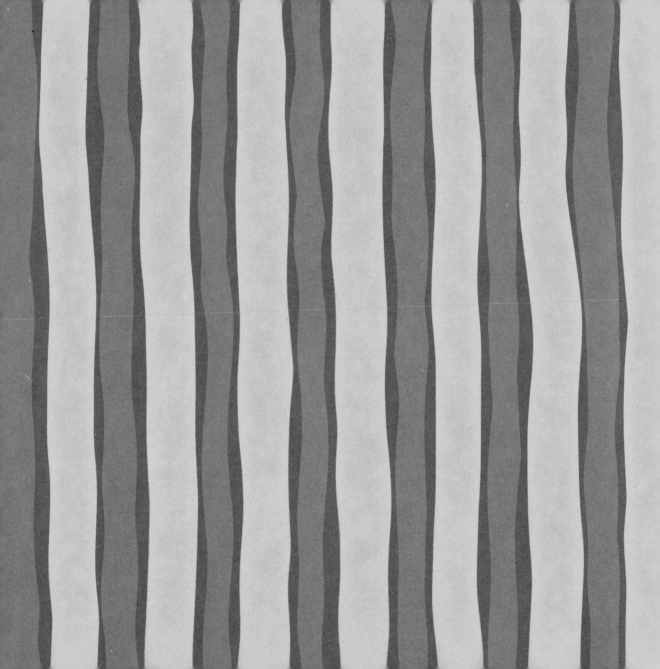